To Serena &
Zara—

Stay Purrrrfect
and Pawesome!

Meow,

Pip

To Pop Sam,
If you were here, I know you would be
teaching me how to find the sweet spot
with my very own set of Sam Bromley
original golf clubs and fussing with me
for playing in the bunkers.

www.mascotbooks.com

Pip's Guide to Ocean City

For more information, please contact:
Mascot Books
620 Herndon Parkway #320
Herndon, VA 20170
info@mascotbooks.com

Library of Congress Control Number: 2019935687

CPSIA Code: PRT0419A
ISBN-13: 978-1-64307-444-3

Printed in the United States

A portion of profits benefit local charities.

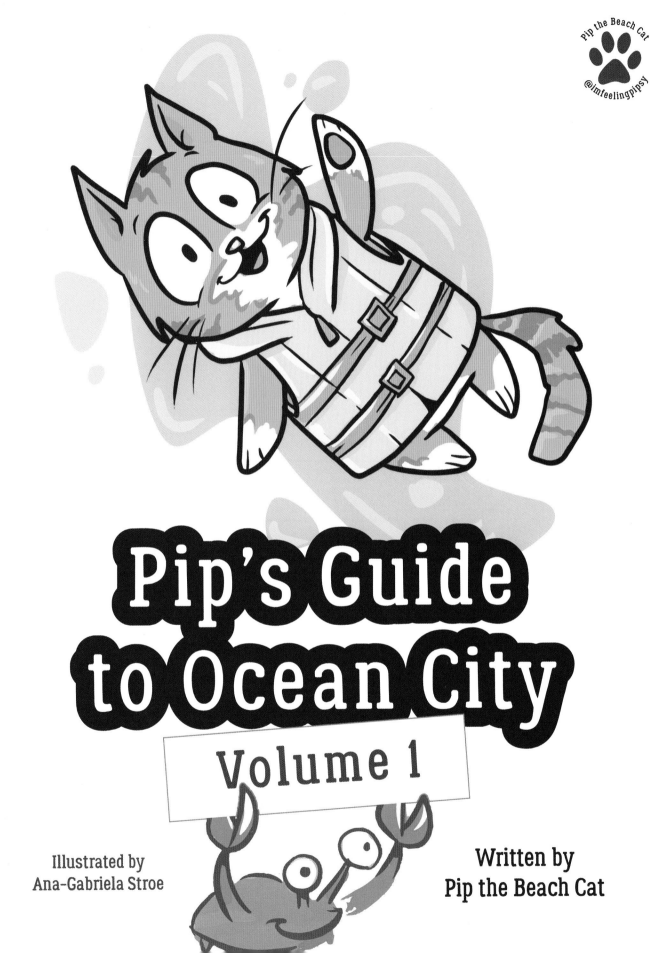

Pip's Guide to Ocean City

Volume 1

Illustrated by
Ana-Gabriela Stroe

Written by
Pip the Beach Cat

Pip the Beach Cat
@imfeelingpipsy

Hi! I'm Pip the Beach Cat! I wasn't always a famous cat. I used to be a dirty little furball wandering the streets of a town called Berlin.

One night there was a really bad storm, so I looked for shelter. A nice family took me in, but couldn't keep me. I was passed around from house to house. No one wanted me.

But then one day, I ended up in Ocean City, and I knew I was finally home.

Ocean City has miles of coastline with the beach on one side and the bay on the other. This means there are tons of activities for you to do when you come to visit!

Every morning, the day begins with a sunrise over the ocean! I love to dig holes and look for sand crabs, build a sandcastle with my friends, search for seashells, or get buried in the sand! Sometimes you can even see dolphins swimming!

The beach is a great place to relax or play. And the ocean's waves are awesome!

A lot of people told me I couldn't or shouldn't go to the beach. A lot of people said, "Cats can't swim!" or, "Cats are afraid of water!" But not me! I love to ride my boogie board and catch waves!

There's more to Ocean City than just the beach. You can ride bicycles with your family, play mini-golf, go to the water park, swim in a pool, go fishing, or ride on a boat! And that's just the beginning!

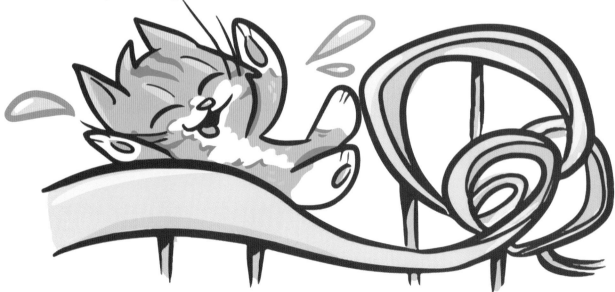

The Ocean City boardwalk is filled with entertainment. You can watch kites fly in the sky, or explore all the nooks and crannies filled with art at the World-Famous Ocean Gallery. You might even find me there and get my pawtograph!

When my tummy starts rumbling, there's lots for me to eat along the boardwalk!

What's your favorite boardwalk food?

After all that eating, I run along the boardwalk until I touch "The Spot!"

When I reach the end of the boardwalk, I can learn all about Ocean City's legends, history, and heroes of life from the Life Saving Museum!

One of my favorite things to do is visit the arcades and rides downtown!

I love to ride the carousel at Trimper's or the Ferris Wheel at Jolly Rogers.

If I'm feeling brave, I might take a ride through The Haunted House or buckle in for the ride of my life on the Tidal Wave rollercoaster!

You can also find me playing skeeball at Playland or posing in the photo booth at Sportland!

On the other side of the island, you can dig your toes into the bottom of the bay and feel for clams, or sit on a dock and go crabbing!

The bayside is a great spot for water sports like paddle boarding, jet skiing, kayaking, or parasailing.

It is also a great way to end your day because you can watch the sun set over the bay.

I hope you have as much fun in Ocean City as I do! And I can't wait to play in the sand with you! Have a great vacation!

Love,

Pip!

About Pip

Pip the Beach Cat resides in Ocean City, Maryland. In his free time, you can find Pip frolicking in the sand by the ocean or riding his stand-up paddle board on the bay. Pip is an active member of his community. He gives back by volunteering at nursing homes across the Eastern Shore, visiting local schools, helping to fundraise for charities, mentoring younger members of his community, fostering homeless kittens, and providing support to families in need. Pip has a significant social media following, where he interacts with his fans daily and gets to know many of them on a personal level. Pip shares his daily adventures on Instagram, Facebook, and TicTok @imfeelingpipsy, and his website, www.pipthebeachcat.com.

In addition to being an author and community volunteer, Pip is also a stuffed animal designer and Official Greeter at many local Ocean City businesses! If you're lucky, you might just get to see him when you are on vacation. Oh yeah, and he loves seafood!

About Pip's Family

Emily Meadows and Jacek Bulak are Pip's caretakers. They live in Ocean City, Maryland, with their three cats Natty, Mowgli, and of course, Pip. Emily is originally from Ocean City and Jacek is from Krakow, Poland. They have enjoyed sharing Pip's journey with the world and hope to one day take Pip over to Europe to meet his grandparents!

Your Memories of Ocean City!